Fine Art Studio

Sculpting

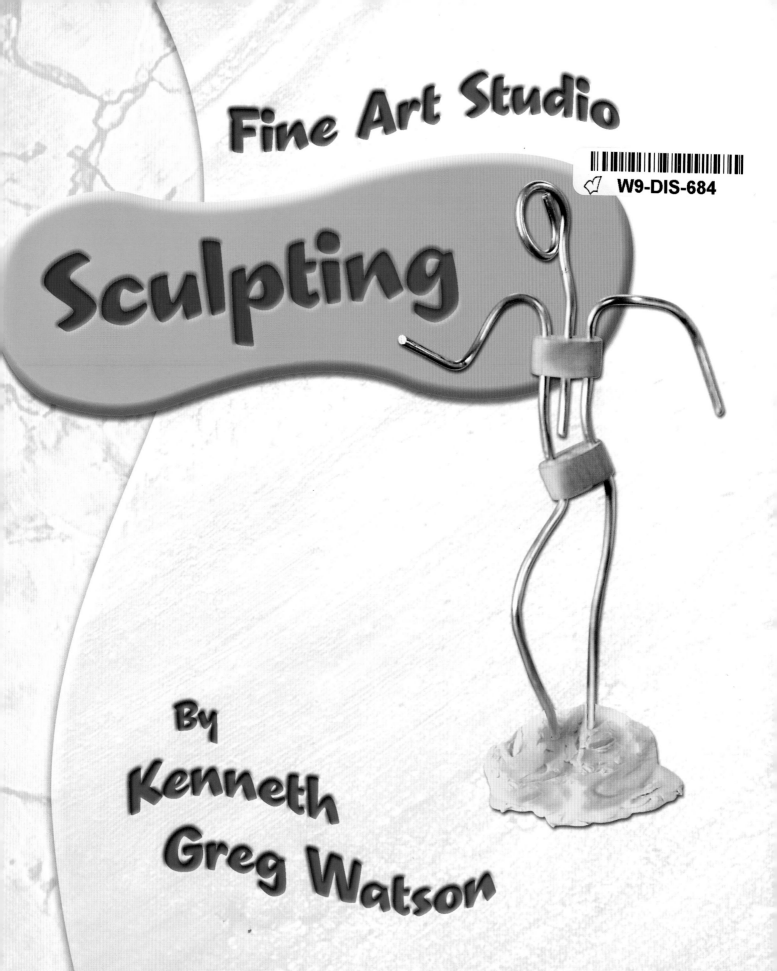

By
Kenneth
Greg Watson

With love for my father,
Kenneth Lowell Watson,
who could make anything.

Silver Dolphin

Silver Dolphin Books
An imprint of the Advantage Publishers Group
5880 Oberlin Drive, San Diego, CA 92121-4794
www.silverdolphinbooks.com

Text copyright © 2004 by becker&mayer!
Fine Art Studio: Sculpting is produced by becker&mayer!,
Bellevue, Washington
www.beckermayer.com

If you have questions or comments about this product, send e-mail to
infobm@beckermayer.com

ISBN-13 : 978-1-59223-329-8
ISBN-10 : 1-59223-329-5
Produced, manufactured, and assembled in China.

5 6 7 8 09 08 07

06391

Edited by Betsy Henry Pringle
Written by Kenneth Greg Watson
Clay sculpting, illustrations, and photographs by Susan Hernday
Art direction by J. Max Steinmetz
Designed by Eddee Helms and J. Max Steinmetz
Design assistance by Karrie Lee
Packaging design by Scott Westgard.
Studio photography by Keith Megay
Product development by Lillis Taylor
Production management by Katie Stephens

Special thanks to: Karen Testa, Mary L. Beebe, Becky Andrews, Lee Mueller, Emma Stower,
Magali Dufour, Barbara Strohl, Dawn Ahlert, Deborah Butterfield, Jennifer Belt, Lindsay Koval,
Cristin O'Keefe Aptowicz, Kristina Bottomley, and Melody Moss.

Image Credits
Every effort has been made to correctly attribute all the material reproduced in this book.
We will be happy to correct any errors in future editions.

Page 3: Illustration of Neolithic horse by Christian Kitzmüller; Cave painting, photo
courtesy of and document elaborated with the support of the French Ministry of Culture
and Communication, Regional Direction for Cultural Affairs–Rhône-Alpes, Regional
Department of Archaeology.

Pages 4–5: Claude Monet, *The Poppy Field*, photo credit: Erich Lessing / Art Resource, NY;
Anthony Howe, *Bigun* and *Rexus*, photographs courtesy of the artist; John Chamberlain,
Untitled, Galleria Nazionale d'Arte Moderna, Rome, Italy, © 2004 Artists Rights Society
(ARS), NY, photo credit: Alinari / Art Resource, NY; Suzanne Averre, *Brown Owl*,
photograph courtesy of the artist; Michelangelo, *David*, photo credit: Scala / Art Resource,
NY; Barbara Hepworth, *Two Forms (Divided Circle)*, photo from the Mary and Leigh Block
Museum of Art, Northwestern University, used with permission.

Pages 6–7: Netsuke, © Christie's Images/CORBIS. Used with permission; Totem pole,
courtesy of the Burke Museum of Natural History and Culture; Auguste Rodin, *The Thinker*,
photo © Kevin McMahan; Deborah Butterfield, *Riot*, photograph courtesy of the artist.

Pages 8–9: Clay soldiers and ushebti, photo credit: Erich Lessing / Art Resource, NY;
Discobolus and Michelangelo, *Pietà*, photo credit: Alinari / Art Resource, NY; Constantin
Brancusi, *Mlle. Pogany I* © 2004 Artists Rights Society (ARS), NY / ADAGP, Paris, photo
credit: Erich Lessing / Art Resource, NY; Edward Tufte, *Escaping Flatland: Willow Shadow 2*,
photo © Graphics Press LLC, used with permission.

Pages 10–11: Don Anderson, *Dancer*, photograph courtesy of the artist; Frédéric-
Auguste Bartholdi, Statue of Liberty, photos © Laurie Platt Winfrey, Inc.

Page 12: Bust of Queen Nefertiti, photo credit: Bildarchiv Preussischer Kulturbesitz / Art
Resource, NY.

Page 20: The Nike of Samothrace, photo credit: Erich Lessing / Art Resource, NY.

Page 26: Edgar Degas, *Fourteen-year-old Dancer*, photo credit: Réunion des Musées
Nationaux / Art Resource, NY.

Page 28: Leonardo da Vinci's horse © the Da Vinci Discovery Center of Science and
Technology; Leonardo da Vinci, Study for the Sforza monument, no. 19 (facsimile), photo
credit: Scala / Art Resource, NY.

Pages 35: Cave painting of horses courtesy of and document elaborated with the
support of the French Ministry of Culture and Communication, Regional Direction for
Cultural Affairs–Rhône-Alpes, Regional Department of Archaeology.

Pages 38–39: Henry Moore, *Three Piece Sculpture: Vertebrae*, reproduced by permission
of the Henry Moore Foundation, photograph courtesy of the Henry Moore Foundation;
Niki de Saint Phalle, *Sun God*, photo from the Stuart Collection, University of California,
San Diego, used with permission; Frédéric-Auguste Bartholdi, Statue of Liberty, photo ©
Laurie Platt Winfrey, Inc.; Alexander Liberman, *Iliad*, photo credit: Nicolas Sapieha / Art
Resource, NY.

Page 40: Don Anderson, *Daphnis*, photograph courtesy of the artist.

Timeless Treasure

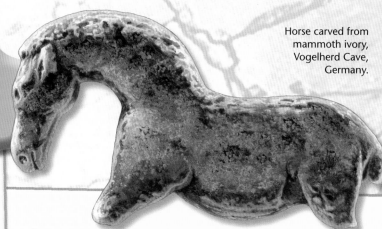

Horse carved from mammoth ivory, Vogelherd Cave, Germany.

Archaeologists are scientists who study the way people lived long ago. Many archaeologists look for scraps of pottery, bone, metal, or stone that were left behind thousands of years ago. Some days, they find something wonderful—something that reminds us that people who lived many ages ago had imagination, wishes, and dreams just like we do.

One of those wonderful days came in Germany in 1975. There, in the darkness of a cave, a tiny sculpture of a horse was found. Someone had spent many hours carving this little horse with a stone knife and a sandstone file. They had even drilled a hole in it so it could be worn as a necklace.

This tiny horse was a treasure to the person who carved it—a two-inch-long masterpiece that any sculptor anytime, anywhere would be proud of.

It was a treasure to the person who wore it. It was probably an amulet, a reminder given to a young person to help him or her think about important things in nature—the strength of a mammoth, the speed of a horse, or the quickness of a bear.

It is a treasure to us. This little horse was made over 30,000 years ago. When the artist who sculpted this little horse lived, almost nothing in life was like what we know today—no electricity, no stores, no farming. No way to live except to hunt with the keen eyes of a saber-toothed tiger, to fish with the skill of a bear, and to protect your children with the courage of a wolf.

But with all those differences and after all that time, this little horse still reaches out to our eyes and hearts. It makes us want to pick it up and feel it. It makes us think of the beautiful and strong horses we have seen running in a field, galloping with a rider, or racing at the Kentucky Derby. The little horse was carved without legs, but that doesn't stop us from imagining it prancing and running. Any good artist leaves something for the imagination.

The artist took his idea of the beauty and movement of a horse and made it real, to share with a young person as a reminder of what they would need to succeed in life. That's what art is, especially sculpture, because it has weight, thickness, and shape like we do. Art is a way to make ideas more real. It was that way 30,000 years ago, and it is still that way today.

Cave painting of a bison from Chauvet-Pont-d'Arc Cave, France.

Table of Contents

The Art of Sculpture

This is a book about art for artists. An artist is anyone who makes art, whether they are famous or not, whether making art is their job or not.

Every culture on earth, now and in the past, has had art. And in most times and places, art has included sculptures of people, animals, and everyday objects.

What Is Sculpture?

Sculpture is art that isn't flat. Most sculptures are made so that they look good from every side.

Claude Monet, *The Poppy Field*, 1873. Oil on canvas, 50 x 65 cm. Musée d'Orsay, Paris, France.

PAINTINGS, DRAWINGS, AND PHOTOGRAPHS HAVE TWO DIMENSIONS: WIDTH AND HEIGHT.

SCULPTURE HAS A THIRD DIMENSION: DEPTH.

When looking at sculpture, ask these questions:

1. What is it made of?
2. Is it realistic or abstract?
3. How was it made?

What Is It Made Of?

Ancient sculptures were made of stone, clay, wood, bone, or ivory. Many small sculptures from long ago were made of glass or gold, and quite a few were made of bronze.

Anthony Howe, *Bigun*. Stainless steel, fiberglass cloth, polyester resin, and urethane paint.

Modern Materials

In the last hundred years or so, the list of things sculptures are made of has gotten longer. If you go into an art gallery or museum showing modern sculpture, you will see pieces made of plastic, fiberglass, aluminum, glass, and wire. You will even find sculpture that looks like it was put together with stuff from a garage sale. Materials like stone, clay, and wood are still being used, too.

John Chamberlain, Untitled, 1965. Painted metal.

Suzanne Averre, *Brown Owl*, 2004. Sand-cast hypertufa with glass eyes.

Great Rivals

Michelangelo and Leonardo da Vinci were great artists and fierce rivals. One time they fought over a block of damaged marble. Michelangelo won, and the block of marble became the masterpiece *David*.

"Eyes watchful . . . the neck of a bull . . . hands of a . . . killer . . . the body, a reservoir of energy. He stands poised to strike."

—Michelangelo describing his statue *David*

Michelangelo, *David*, 1501. Detail of head in profile. Marble. Accademia, Florence, Italy.

Is It Realistic or Abstract?

A lot of art copies the way something in real life looks. This type of art makes people say, "Oh, that is a good likeness of the president." This type of art is realistic.

But not all art is that way. Often, artists don't put in every little part of what something looks like, maybe because they want you to notice the parts they think are most important, or maybe they want to make something look like it's moving very fast when it isn't moving at all.

Lincoln Memorial, Washington, D.C.

Barbara Hepworth

One of the most famous abstract sculptors of the middle twentieth century was Barbara Hepworth (1903–1975). Hepworth said that sculptors should think about more than just the surface of their work. One of her inventions, quickly picked up by other artists, was the idea of putting a window or hole through a large sculpture so that whatever was in the background became part of the design. The same sculpture can look very different if the view through the hole is a white-walled gallery, a green hillside, or a crowded sidewalk.

Abstract Art

Abstract art comes partly from the artist's imagination. Abstract art can sometimes involve creating shapes and textures that have nothing to do with "real life." This is also called *nonobjective* art.

Most sculpture, even the most realistic, has some abstraction to it, if only because no piece of art can be an exact copy of its subject.

Anthony Howe, *Rexus*, 2002. Stainless steel.

Barbara Hepworth, *Two Forms (Divided Circle)*, 1969. Cast bronze with green-brown patina, 96 x 90 x 30 inches. Mary and Leigh Block Museum of Art, Northwestern University, gift of Leigh B. Block, 1988.

How Was It Made?

You can also describe a sculpture by the way it was made and what tools the artist used. The three main ways sculptures are made are by *carving*, *modeling*, and *assembling*.

1. Carving

When carving, the artist starts with a piece of material (such as wood, stone, clay, or a bar of soap) and takes parts away using knives, chisels, saws, dynamite (yes, if you are carving the side of a mountain), and other tools until what's left is the shape the artist imagined for the sculpture.

Carving is also called *subtractive* sculpture because you are taking things away. The hard thing about subtractive sculpture is that you have to be very careful not to carve away too much.

Totem Poles

For centuries, Native Americans on the northwestern coast of North America carved huge wooden sculptures, often called totem poles. These massive cedar logs with figures of humans and animals depict stories of important ancestors. Each family has its own designs that others can't use, sort of like a company logo or the coat of arms of a European knight.

Model of Chief Skulka's Totem Pole, courtesy of the Burke Museum of Natural History and Culture, Catalog #2.5E536.

Netsuke

Not all important sculptures are big. Some of the finest sculptures made by Japanese artists were netsuke (net-SOO-kay), little masterpieces of carved stone, wood, ivory, or fired clay. Made during the age of the samurai (1000–1860), netsuke were fashioned to hang from a kimono sash. Some netsuke are only an inch long, but they have details you can only see close up or with a magnifying glass.

Ivory netsuke, signed by Mitsuharu, 18th century.

2. Modeling

Modeling starts with pieces of material that can be mashed together and molded to get the shapes the artist imagined. Wax and clay are popular modeling materials.

Because the main idea of this kind of sculpture is to put pieces together and mold them into a bigger shape, this is called *additive* sculpture. Most of the projects that you will be doing with this kit will be made this way.

Auguste Rodin, *The Thinker*, 1880. Bronze, 182.9 x 98.4 x 142.2 cm. Musée Rodin, Paris, France.

The Thinker

Modeled in 1880 by Auguste Rodin (Row-DAHN), The Thinker *shows a man sitting down, leaning forward, and resting his chin on one hand. He is not paying attention to anything except whatever is on his mind. Perhaps it is meant to remind us that the work we do with our brains is as important as the work we do with our bodies.*

Rodin once got into trouble because he was such a good sculptor. One of his bronze men looked so real that some people thought he had made a mold around a real person and then somehow slipped the man out and poured bronze into the cast. Eventually, everyone understood that Rodin had modeled the figure in wax.

Pipes to Ponies

Sometimes the parts of an assembled sculpture look like what they were before they were used to make the sculpture. This horse sculpture by Deborah Butterfield is a good example. Although it is horse-shaped and realistically shows the way a horse stands, it isn't hard to see that it has been put together from pieces of metal.

Born on the day of the Kentucky Derby horse race, sculptor Deborah Butterfield has been fascinated by horses her whole life. She almost became a veterinarian instead of an artist. Her assembled horses are made from metals, wire, and wood.

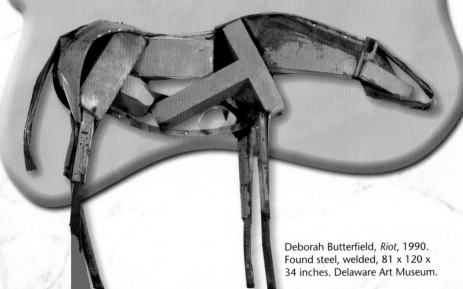

Deborah Butterfield, *Riot*, 1990. Found steel, welded, 81 x 120 x 34 inches. Delaware Art Museum.

3. Assembling

In assembly, the artist puts together different pieces to make larger shapes; however, unlike modeling, in assembly the individual parts keep their shapes and textures.

Sometimes the parts are made to fit carefully together so that the finished sculpture looks like it is all one piece. The Statue of Liberty is a good example—her outside is made of hundreds of sheets of metal that were hammered, folded, and shaped so that, when all put together over a framework, they look like a woman wearing a long robe and carrying a torch.

Sculpture throughout History

No one knows how long people have been making sculptures. The Face of Borzone, a large rock found in Italy that resembles a human face, is believed to be over 150,000 years old. Did Stone Age humans carve it? Some archaeologists believe so.

About 20,000 years ago, someone in what is now Afghanistan carved a limestone pebble to show two circle eyes, a lumpy nose, a beard, and a moustache. Why was it made and what was it used for? We will probably never know.

Clay Warriors

Life-size clay soldiers from the tomb of the first emperor of a united China, Qin Shihuangdi. Archaeological site excavated 1974. Xian, China.

More than 1,250 years ago, 700,000 people worked for three years to make a larger-than-life-size clay army for Qin Shihuangdi, the first Chinese emperor. Thousands of soldiers and horses were built to serve and guard the emperor in death. Workers digging a well in the city of Xian in 1974 found an underground vault filled with row after row of figures. Each soldier was a fine sculpture with its own face, body position, armor, and weapons, standing ready to serve. Even today, not all of the army—which stretches over more than 10 acres—has been uncovered.

Ancient Egyptians

Ushebti box, three wooden ushebtis, servants for the deceased in the hereafter, 21st dynasty. Third intermediate period (1080–714 BC). Louvre, Paris, France.

The ancient Egyptians sculpted tiny mummy-shaped statues, called *ushebti*. It was believed that the ushebti could perform certain tasks for the dead. When an important person died, ushebti that resembled the person were buried along with the mummy.

The Greeks and Romans

Myron of Athens (5th century BC), Discobolus. Museo Nazionale Romano (Terme di Diocleziano), Rome, Italy.

Ancient Greeks and Romans admired beautiful, healthy human bodies—they imagined their gods as looking like the best of humans, but more so. Many people think that realistic "classical" Greek sculpture is the starting point of everything good about European and American art. Surely, it is true that few artists of any age have matched the strong poses and careful detail of these masterpieces.

An Artistic Revolution

The Renaissance

Michelangelo, *Pietà*, 1498–1499. Marble. St. Peter's Basilica, Vatican State.

Until about 500 years ago, being an artist in Europe was just another job, like being a blacksmith. But then something happened called the Renaissance (REN-uh-sahns). The word *renaissance* means "rebirth," and the Renaissance was a time when people started to seek new knowledge about science and exploration, and they began to look at the art and writings left from old cultures like the Greeks and Romans.

Artists saw that the ancient Greeks had made sculptures that looked more real and alive than anything that had been made in Europe for hundreds of years, and they began to copy them and learn from them.

During the Renaissance, it became a status symbol for wealthy people and important families to own a beautiful piece of art. Soon, the best artists began to be asked for by name—Raphael, Cellini, Michelangelo, and Leonardo da Vinci. Being an artist had become something special.

Constantin Brancusi, *Mlle. Pogany I,* 1912–13. Plaster, 44 x 24.5 x 30.5 cm. Musée National d'Art Moderne, Centre Georges Pompidou, Paris, France.

After the Renaissance, sculptors continued to make sculptures that copied the Greeks. The men who paid the artists formed clubs, called academies, to make sure artists followed the "rules." Creativity was not encouraged.

But starting in the 1800s, things began to change. There were fewer kings and queens, and everyday people were running the governments. More and more people could read and travel, and that got them curious to try new things.

Artists began experimenting. They bent shapes to show movement and feeling. They made sculptures of ordinary people, to show that their lives were important, too. They looked at art from other cultures. They started to let their own imaginations be more important than just copying what had already been done.

The people who bought art started to notice the new energy of these artists. The academies became less important. What became more important was the idea of the artist as a unique person with his own vision.

Sculpture Today

Edward Tufte, *Escaping Flatland: Willow Shadow 2.* Stainless steel, two units, 12 feet high and covering an area approximately 15 x 30 feet.

Today in sculpture, the artist's imagination is the only limit. There are people who work with bulldozers to shape the ground into sculptures; others wrap whole buildings in fabric or use beams of light instead of marble or wires. And there are sculptors who make little stone animals that the people who made the horse 30,000 years ago would understand. It all comes from someone's imagination being turned into something real. They are all artists, and so are you.

ARTY FACT
Michelangelo was barely over 20 when he finished the Pietà. On the day he delivered the sculpture, he overheard a spectator say that Michelangelo was too young to have created such a magnificent piece of work. In a fit of fury, the artist returned that night and chiseled his name onto the statue. He later regretted this and it is the only work Michelangelo ever signed.

What Is Art?

All art starts in the imagination of the artist. Making something real that starts in your imagination is called *creativity*. Even if something is a close copy of a real person or a sunset, an artist has to imagine how to turn the living face into a bunch of clay pieces pushed together just so, or how to turn a sunset into brushstrokes of color on a canvas. Imagination is even more important if the art is purely abstract and isn't a likeness of anything but an idea.

All real art is something new. This is called being *original*. If you make something with no imagination of your own—if you copy something else or copy another artist's way of working—you aren't really making art, because there's nothing in it that belongs only to you.

Art is, partly, about the artist sharing something he or she thinks is important and hoping other people think so too. Sometimes, the message is simple: "Look at this statue—this guy was important!" Sometimes art tells complicated stories, like the way the artist feels when she listens to her favorite music.

Art doesn't have to have a job other than its message. Sometimes art is also a chair or a warm cover for your bed, but often, it's just art—a painting, sculpture, photograph, or drawing.

Don Anderson,
Dancer, 2003.
Welded stainless steel.

The Clay Sculptor's Tools

Clay

Your clay, called *plasticine* (PLASS-tuh-seen), comes in three colors: white, terra-cotta (orange), and ocher (yellow). There is enough white clay to make a large horse in all one color. Plasticine does not dry out, so you will be able to use this clay over and over again.

Cogs

You will use your six cogs in a variety of ways to build sculptures. The armature wires fit into and through the holes of the cogs.

Shaping Tools

Use your double-ended clay-shaping tools to cut, scrape, and add details.

Armature Wires

Clay sculptures are often heavy. They need something strong inside them to help them stand up and hold their shape, much like the skeleton in your body or the steel beams in a skyscraper. This something is called an *armature*. Your kit comes with nine bendable wires that can be used in a variety of ways to pose and support your art.

Statue of Liberty, wood and plaster model of hand.

STEEL AND WOOD
Workers used wood and steel to build the armature inside the Statue of Liberty.

9 ARMATURE WIRES

Statue of Liberty skeleton, torch, and head in Paris, 1883.

Optional Tools

PAPER CLIP

COMB

TOOTHPICKS

HOMEMADE TOOL

ALUMINUM FOIL

TIP
Find or make custom tools that suit your needs. A paper clip is good for scooping away clay, an old plastic comb is good for creating hair texture, and your fingers make the best tools for smoothing and pushing clay into shape.

Setting Up Your Work Area

Create an area where you can work undisturbed. You will need a work surface or table and good light. To protect your work surface, it's a good idea to have an old cookie sheet, a plastic tablecloth, or a plastic cutting board (perhaps from a yard sale) to roll your clay on.

CLEANUP
Liquid soap and warm water will remove the clay from your hands and other surfaces.

11

Seeing Like an Artist

On the following pages, you will see how one artist made a portrait using the same clay and tools that came with this book. This doesn't mean that your work should look just like the examples in the pictures—one of the great things about art is that each artist's work is different! Use these ideas to make the art you see in your imagination.

Let's get started!

Bust of
Queen Nefertit
From the workshop
Thutmosis. Egypt, 18t
dynasty. Painted limestone

The Job of an Artist

Your main job as an artist is to look at things more carefully than other people, to really see and think about what is around you, then to share what you find by making art. Try practicing this kind of careful seeing as you do this project. Making a portrait of a human face is one of the best ways to practice seeing—and thinking about what you see—because there's always a lot going on in a face.

Meet the Model

For the portrait model, you will use the face you know best of all, your own! Your first sculpture may not turn out looking much like you, but by the time you're done, you'll know quite a bit about the way faces are put together.

Ancient Perfection

The ancient Egyptians made fine sculptures, especially of their pharaohs, or rulers, and their families. One of the most famous Egyptian sculptures is a portrait head of Queen Nefertiti, who lived about 3,400 years ago. Nefertiti, whose name means "the beautiful (or perfect) woman," was the stepmother of Tutankhamen (King Tut). Egyptians wanted their art to look as if it would last forever, so the poses and expressions are often stiff.

MATERIALS

- 1 OVAL COG
- 2 SHORT WIRES
- 1 BLOCK OF CLAY (ANY COLOR)
- ALUMINUM FOIL

TiP Don't worry about making your sculptures the "right" colors. Most sculptures in museums and art galleries are the color of the materials used to make them—wood, stone, clay, bronze, and so on. Painting is the art of color, but sculpture is the art of shape and texture and the way shapes fit together.

Before You Begin

Set Up Your Mirrors

Set up a large mirror and a chair where you are going to work. A second mirror that you can hold in your hand will help you see your sides and back better.

looking at back & sides of head

with two mirrors

Looking in mirror at self

HERE'S LOOKING AT YOU!

Making sure you can see your face, neck, and shoulders in the mirror, look at yourself for a minute or two. Actively look—don't be in a hurry. Remember that one of the most important steps in making art is looking at things, and really seeing what you look at.

A lot of people doing sculpture for the first time make the face flat, with the eyes, nose, and mouth stuck on like refrigerator magnets! You can do better when you take the time to really see what you're looking at.

- *The face isn't flat—it's part of the whole, round head.*
- *Eyes are in hollow areas that angle in from the front and sides of the face.*
- *In the middle of each eye socket, the eye and eyelid poke out like part of a ball.*
- *Chins stick out in the middle.*
- *Cheeks can be round, bony, or flat under each eye.*
- *Eyebrows sit on the bony part of your forehead above the eye socket.*
- *Ears and noses are different on every face.*

A Little Rule of Thumb about Proportions

EYES: Halfway between the top of the head and the tip of the chin. The distance between the eyes is equal to the width of one eye.

NOSE: Center of face. The nose length is about one-quarter the length of the head. The width of both nostrils together is the same width as one eye.

EARS: Extend from the eyebrows down to the tip of the nose.

LIPS: Located between the bottom tip of the nose and the tip of the chin. The corners of the mouth line up with the eye centers.

NECK: About one-half the size of the head.

½

½

DID YOU KNOW?

Many people place the eyes way up at the top, and the mouth way down at the bottom. In real faces, most children's eyes are just about halfway between the very top of the head and the very bottom of the chin (most adults' eyes are a little higher than halfway up, but not much). Most people's eyes are a little closer to the centerline of the nose than the side of the head.

TIP You might want to make notes or draw a sketch of your face and the side of your head so that you will get the proportions you want in the sculpture.

13

Making Your Portrait

Front   **Side**

① Build the Armature

Bend one of the short wires into a lightbulb shape and press the ends into holes 1 and 5 of an oval cog.

Bend a second wire into a *lopsided* lightbulb shape and press the ends into holes 2 and 4 of the cog—this wire will cross the first wire at the top of the portrait head. The shape doesn't need to be precise.

5   2   4

YOU MAY WANT TO TAPE THE COG TO YOUR WORK SURFACE SO IT DOESN'T TIP OVER.

Finished Armature

Foil

② Foil

Crumple up a 10-inch square piece of aluminum foil and push it into the space between the two loops of wire on the armature.

The foil needs to be squished in so that it isn't bigger than the armature wires. This way, you don't have to use your clay to fill up this space (which saves clay!) and your sculpture won't be as heavy (which is important when you build large sculptures).

USE ANOTHER SQUARE OF FOIL TO COVER THE ENTIRE ARMATURE.

③ Cover the Armature

Start covering the armature with small, flat lumps of clay, pushing and smoothing them together with your fingers or a tool. Make a thick enough layer all over so that you can carve out the eyes, neck, and other features without hitting the armature or the foil.

④ Roughing In

Build up more clay on the areas where your own head stands out—your cheeks, chin, and the back of the head above the neck. Check the shape of your head in the mirror as you work. Artists call this part *roughing in*.

TiP Don't worry about details like lips or eyelids yet—your portrait will be better if you get the main shapes right first.

Add or cut away clay to get the rough shape of the portrait head right. That is one great thing about using clay for sculpture—if you were carving wood or stone, it would be very hard to put a piece back once you had cut it away!

⑤ Score the Proportions

Use your knife tool to draw a shallow line down the front of the head, and draw side-to-side lines where the eyebrows, eyes, nose, and mouth will be. Look at your own face and the proportion drawing to get these right.

Making Faces

Now you are ready to start working on the face. Even though a small portrait like the one you are making doesn't have space for tiny detail, spend plenty of time sculpting features such as the eyes, nose, and mouth. These features say the most about us.

⑥ Scoop Out the Eye Sockets

Use a paper clip or other tool to scoop some clay out of the eye socket areas—not too deep! Eye sockets extend out into the sides of the head— they aren't just dents in the front of your face.

TiP For most people, the part of the face where the eye is doesn't come out nearly as far as the eyebrow area above and the cheek below. Use the mirror to see how this is on your face. In the middle of this low spot is the eye; it is round, like part of a ball that sticks out just a little.

⑦ Add the Nose

Take a pea-sized lump of clay and roll it into a stubby coil or "snake" about ½ inch long.

Pinch

Spread

Slice clay back if too

IF THE NOSE IS TOO BIG, SLICE SOME CLAY OFF THE BACK.

Pinch this coil into a long triangle shape and attach it to the middle of the face. Smooth the sides of the triangle into the face slightly.

On most people, there is a little low area across the top of the nose. Use the club-shaped tool to press in this area and to smooth the sides of the carved-out eye socket areas.

⑧ Add the Lips

Cut a ½-inch-long piece of thinly rolled clay and press it gently under the nose. Smooth it into the clay of the face along the top and outside edges.

Add another piece just below and smooth it on the bottom and outside edges. This is because your lips are part of your face, not just wormy shapes under your nose.

Use the pointed and club-shaped tools in the kit to shape the curves of the lips after they are in place.

⑨ Add Cheeks and Brows

Add little pads of clay under the eyes and smooth them into the face to make cheekbones.

Add a tiny worm of clay above each eye socket to build up the brow area.

Smooth the clay.

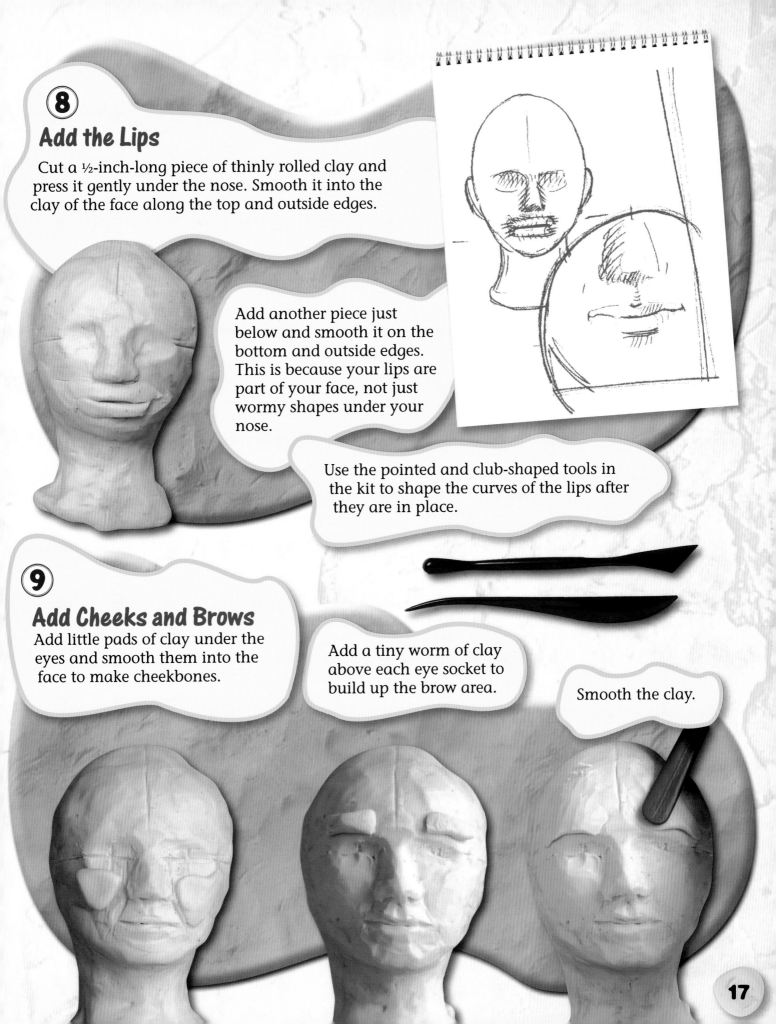

10 The Ears

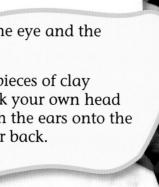

roll   flatten

Score the sides of the head at the top of the eye and the bottom of the nose.

Start the ears with two teardrop-shaped pieces of clay flattened onto the sides of the head. Check your own head to get the ear size and shape right. Smooth the ears onto the side of the head in front, but not the top or back.

11 Insert the Eyeballs

Press a pea-sized (or smaller) ball of clay into the center of each eye socket area. The ball should be small enough that it doesn't fill up the scooped-out area. Use a round-ended tool to smooth out the edges of the ball.

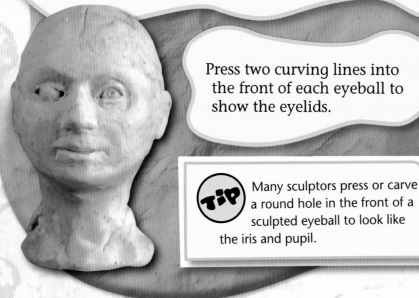

Press two curving lines into the front of each eyeball to show the eyelids.

TIP Many sculptors press or carve a round hole in the front of a sculpted eyeball to look like the iris and pupil.

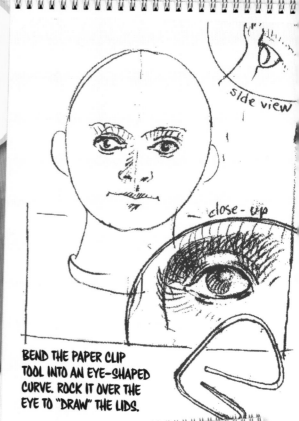

side view

close-up

BEND THE PAPER CLIP TOOL INTO AN EYE-SHAPED CURVE. ROCK IT OVER THE EYE TO "DRAW" THE LIDS.

Paper clip tool to make nostrils

12 Add Details

Use pointed and rounded tools to shape some of the smaller lines and features on the face. You can't catch every detail, so work on the things that are most obvious when you look in the mirror.

(13) Hair

Look at yourself in the mirror, then gently add flat pads or thin ropes of clay to the same areas of your sculpted head where you have a lot of hair. Don't smooth these pads down—let them hang off the portrait where your hair sticks out.

Use a comb or toothpick to show the texture of the hair in some places, but not everywhere. If you have a buzz cut, just texture the surface of the head. Eyebrows can be tiny snakes of clay, given texture with a quick tap of the comb or some small lines with a toothpick. If you don't have heavy eyebrows, maybe a couple of quick scratches above the eyes will be enough.

(14) Smoothing

When you have finished shaping the hair and features of your portrait, go back and smooth some areas of "skin." Place a sheet of plastic wrap gently down on the surface and roll one of your curved tools over the area you want to smooth. When you pull the plastic away, the area underneath will be very smooth.

Finished? Yes!

Stop and ask yourself—is it done? This sounds like a silly question, but you can make art look worse, not better, if you keep working just because you think it's not perfect or even because it's fun. If you are satisfied with your little portrait, you might want to place it on a pedestal for all the world to see!

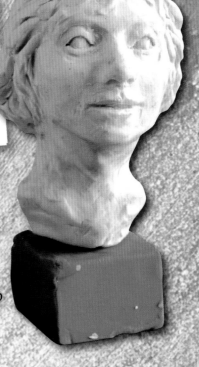

Pose and Proportion

The Nike of Samothrace, goddess of victory, circa 190 BC. Marble. Louvre, Paris, France.

To sculpt a human figure, you will use many of the skills you learned while making a portrait. In this project, you are going to concentrate on *pose* and *proportion* and not as much on fine details like lips and eyes.

Hold That Pose!

Many artists who make figure sculptures use a model when they work. The artist tells the model how to pose—how to stand or sit or hold her head and arms for the sculpture being made. You might ask a friend or family member to be your model. The best thing would be to work with someone else who wants to make sculptures, so you can take turns being each other's models!

TIP Choose a place to work where you won't be disturbed and where you have good, clear light to see the model and the sculpture. Make sketches of your model from more than one direction before starting to work with the clay. This way, you can see the pose all the way around as you work (and maybe you can do some work when the model isn't there).

Classically Carved

A famous example of carving is an 11-foot-tall marble statue of a woman with birdlike wings. This statue was dug out of the ground in 1863 on the Greek island of Samothrace. She was probably carved about 2,200 years ago, and even though her head and arms were broken off and lost many centuries ago, she is still one of the most beautiful, carefully carved statues in the world. This statue, now in the Louvre museum in Paris, is called the Nike of Samothrace, or Winged Victory. One of the Victory's hands was dug up in 1950, and now rests in its own case near the statue.

SITTINGS

A good clay figure sculpture will take a couple of sessions with the model holding a pose while the sculptor works. These modeling sessions are called sittings. Many artists make sketches (quick drawings) to help them remember things they will need to know for their work.

MATERIALS

- 2 ROUND COGS
- 2 LONG WIRES
- 1 SHORT WIRE
- ALUMINUM FOIL
- 2 BLOCKS OF CLAY (CAN BE DIFFERENT COLORS)
- TAPE
- MARKER
- RULER (OPTIONAL)
- SKETCH PAPER (OPTIONAL)

① Build the Armature

Begin your figure sculpture by assembling the wires and cogs to make "bones" for the sculpture.

First, make a small loop at the end of the short piece of wire. This will be the head. Poke the unbent end of this wire through the center hole of a round cog. Let the wire stick up far enough to make the head and neck, as shown below.

Take two long wires and put them into opposite holes on the same cog. This cog is going to be the armature for the upper chest. Leave enough wire sticking out beside the looped head to bend down and make arms, wrists, and hands.

THE PART OF A PERSON'S (OR A SCULPTURE'S) BODY FROM THE SHOULDERS TO THE HIPS IS CALLED THE *TORSO*.

Tip: Once you have moved the cog where you want it, use your thumb to gently press the wire near the cog. By bending the wire just a little, you can hold the cog in place. If the cog still slips, wrap a small piece of tape around the wire on both sides of the cog.

Next, poke the lower parts of these two wires through two holes in another cog. Push the wires through until the second cog is in place to be the armature for the hips of your figure.

② Proportion Drawing

Now, look at the proportion drawing to decide where your sculpture's knees and elbows will bend. This will make a big difference in how good the finished sculpture looks.

Mark joint with a pen.

elbows

elbows

$\frac{1}{2}$

knees

⚠ BASES AND PEDESTALS

Some sculptures in museums and galleries sit right on the ground, but most of them have bases. A tall base is called a pedestal. A base or pedestal raises up the sculpture and makes people notice it and think of it as something special. It also keeps people from bumping into the sculpture and knocking it over.

Tip: If your figure sculpture is going to stand up straight or stay in a pose that looks like it's moving, it will need a base.

Take a big blob of clay (any color) and stick the legs into it. You will be picking up the sculpture as you work on it, so the blob will be a handy holder.

21

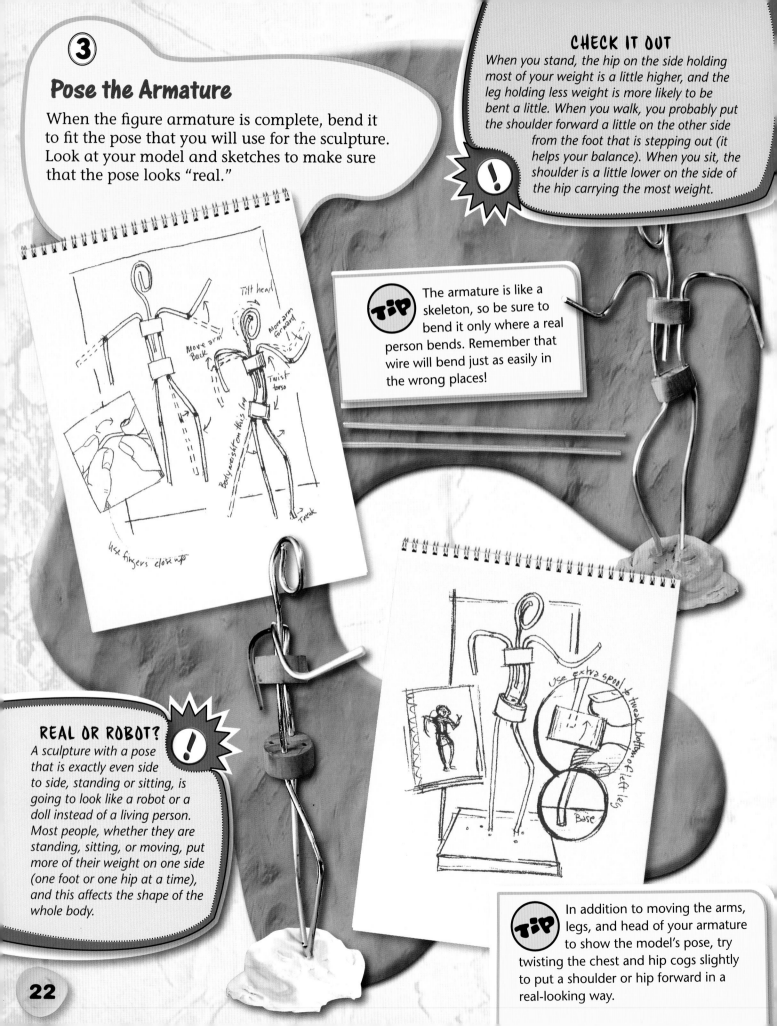

③

Pose the Armature

When the figure armature is complete, bend it to fit the pose that you will use for the sculpture. Look at your model and sketches to make sure that the pose looks "real."

CHECK IT OUT

When you stand, the hip on the side holding most of your weight is a little higher, and the leg holding less weight is more likely to be bent a little. When you walk, you probably put the shoulder forward a little on the other side from the foot that is stepping out (it helps your balance). When you sit, the shoulder is a little lower on the side of the hip carrying the most weight.

TIP The armature is like a skeleton, so be sure to bend it only where a real person bends. Remember that wire will bend just as easily in the wrong places!

REAL OR ROBOT?

A sculpture with a pose that is exactly even side to side, standing or sitting, is going to look like a robot or a doll instead of a living person. Most people, whether they are standing, sitting, or moving, put more of their weight on one side (one foot or one hip at a time), and this affects the shape of the whole body.

TIP In addition to moving the arms, legs, and head of your armature to show the model's pose, try twisting the chest and hip cogs slightly to put a shoulder or hip forward in a real-looking way.

④ Apply Foil to the Armature

Fill the area between the two cogs with crumpled foil, and then wrap this middle area with foil.

Wrap 3 x 6-inch pieces of foil around each arm and leg, keeping in mind that arms and legs are larger near the torso. Squeeze these foil pieces down firmly to the wire armature.

Thread some foil through the head coil and form a head and neck. Don't make the head very large—you can add clay later to get it the right size.

Use another 3 x 6-inch piece of foil around the shoulders and back. You are basically adding the "muscles" to your armature "skeleton."

The armature must fit completely inside the clay sculpture, so make sure there are no cogs, wires, or pieces of foil sticking out.

Wrap foil around arm

⑤ Add Clay

Begin adding clay to the completed armature. Make a ball about the size of a walnut for each leg. Take one ball and roll it into a baseball-bat shape as long as the leg of your sculpture. Press this over the foil, starting on the outside of the leg. Press the clay all around the armature in an even layer.

Add small pieces to complete the rough shape of the leg if you need to. If you are going to make a foot, leave some extra clay at the bottom. You don't have to worry about feet if you are going to keep your figure in the blob of clay.

Moosh & Pinch

Extra for foot

Adding clay coils to limbs

⑥ Cover the Head, Neck, and Torso

Continue covering the armature. Pinch out small, flat pieces to cover the head, neck, and torso. Use a piece about the size of a big grape to cover each arm. Roll these pieces out and press the baseball-bat shape all the way around the armature.

⑦ Smooth and Shape the Clay

In places where your fingers are too big, use tools to smooth the clay into place. Twirling the club-shaped tool like you would a rolling pin is good for this. Don't worry about any details yet—look at your model and sketches and add enough clay to shape the pose you want. Add extra bits of clay and smooth them in as needed, such as on the back of the head, the chin, the shoulders, and the buttocks.

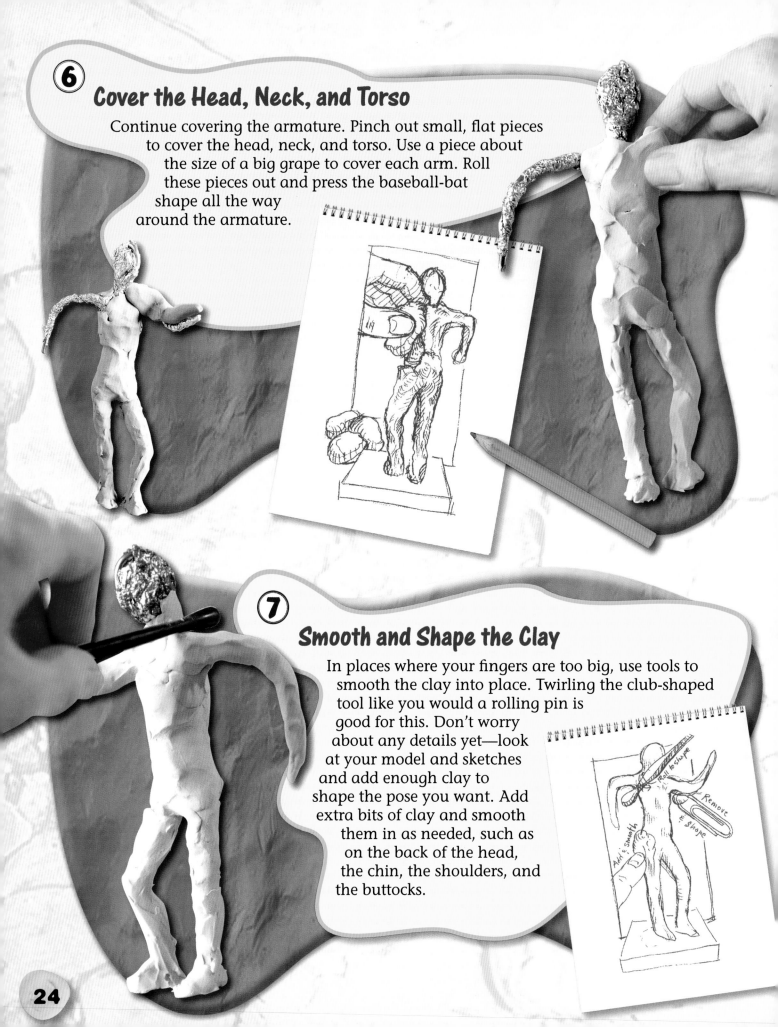

⑧ Check the Proportions

When the roughing in is finished, use the knife tool to draw a line that follows the center of the body from the neck to the hips. Then draw cross lines at the center of the chest, the top of the hips, and the belly button.

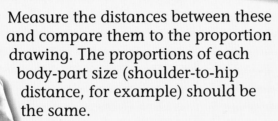

Measure the distances between these and compare them to the proportion drawing. The proportions of each body-part size (shoulder-to-hip distance, for example) should be the same.

A line drawn where the backbone would be can help you see if you have built the sculpture too heavy or too light on one side.

⑨ Add and Subtract Clay

Add clay as needed. If you need to subtract clay from an area to make the pose look good, or if there is too much clay in a spot (like under an arm), use a paper clip or a bent piece of wire to scoop away the extra clay.

Tip

Before scooping away more than a tiny bit of clay, use a toothpick to poke into the clay and see how close you are to the foil or armature in that spot.

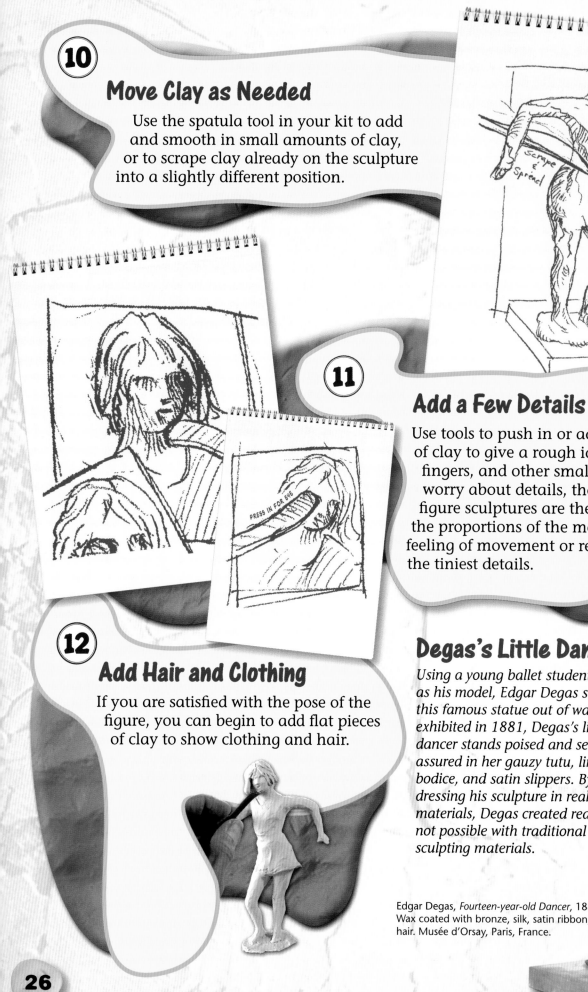

⑩ Move Clay as Needed

Use the spatula tool in your kit to add and smooth in small amounts of clay, or to scrape clay already on the sculpture into a slightly different position.

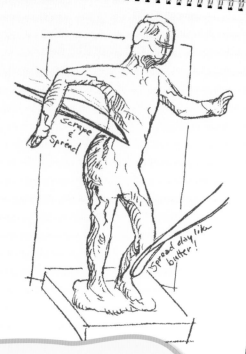

⑪ Add a Few Details

Use tools to push in or add small amounts of clay to give a rough idea of the face, fingers, and other small body parts. Don't worry about details, though. The best figure sculptures are the ones that show the proportions of the model's pose and the feeling of movement or rest, not the ones with the tiniest details.

⑫ Add Hair and Clothing

If you are satisfied with the pose of the figure, you can begin to add flat pieces of clay to show clothing and hair.

Degas's Little Dancer

Using a young ballet student in Paris as his model, Edgar Degas sculpted this famous statue out of wax. First exhibited in 1881, Degas's little dancer stands poised and self-assured in her gauzy tutu, linen bodice, and satin slippers. By dressing his sculpture in real materials, Degas created realism not possible with traditional sculpting materials.

Edgar Degas, *Fourteen-year-old Dancer*, 1881. Wax coated with bronze, silk, satin ribbon, and hair. Musée d'Orsay, Paris, France.

(13)

Look at All Sides

Continue to look at the sculpture from all sides. Compare it with your model by walking around her or him and by looking at any sketches you made from different angles.

SHOWING MOTION

In an action pose like the one shown, getting the shapes (not the details) of the hair and clothing is often more important than the face. Why? Showing the way hair and clothes look when we move is one of the best ways to show the idea of motion in a stationary sculpture. Remember that long hair and hanging cloth moves in curves, with the bottom edge following behind.

(!)

TIP Remember—the most important things in this project are proportion and pose.

Fabulous!

Your sculpture won't look just like this example and it might not look just like your model. But now you know how artists make interesting and lively figure sculptures!

Form Follows Function

This time, you will work with a model that is a little less "everyday" for most of us, unless you live near a horse ranch!

The horse photos in your kit will be your model. Use the different views the way you would walk around a model who is standing or sitting in the room with you.

As with any sculpture, begin by spending some time looking at your model and letting yourself really see what is there.

Leonardo da Vinci's horse, Milan, Italy. Photograph courtesy of the Da Vinci Discovery Center of Science and Technology.

Leonardo's Horse

This horse sculpture waited five hundred years to be built. Why? About 1485, the duke of Milan decided to have a bronze horse sculpted. Leonardo da Vinci wanted the job of making this horse—it would be his masterpiece.

Leonardo got the job, but the duke kept changing his mind. The delays stretched out for years, as the sculpture was designed and redesigned. Finally, in 1493, Leonardo sculpted a full-size clay model of the horse. The duke was happy, the artist was happy. But more time went by, and in the meantime the duke made a cannon with the bronze that was meant for the sculpture. In 1499, the French invaded Italy and the duke ran away. French archers used Leonardo's massive clay model for target practice. Leonardo was sad about the horse for the rest of his life.

In the 1990s, an American art collector and artist named Charles Dent employed a young American sculptor named Nina Akamu to sculpt the horse using Leonardo's surviving drawings. It would be a gift from America to the Italian people. After "only" a few years, the 24-foot-high horse was finished and cast in bronze. It was unveiled in Milan exactly five hundred years after the French shot their arrows at Leonardo's giant clay model.

Leonardo made sketch after sketch of real horses so that his statue would look like it was alive.

Leonardo da Vinci, study for the Sforza monument, no. 19 (facsimile). Gabinetto dei Disegni e delle Stampe, Uffizi, Florence, Italy.

MATERIALS

- HORSE PHOTOS IN YOUR PORTFOLIO ENVELOPE
- 2 ROUND COGS
- 3 LONG WIRES
- 2 BLOCKS OF CLAY
- ALUMINUM FOIL
- TOOLS
- PAPER CLIP

Understanding Horses

Horses are mammals, like human beings. But a horse doesn't stand or move like a human. For example, what looks like a knee on a horse's front leg is the same joint as your wrist.

EARS
Horses' ears can swivel around to catch the sounds of their herd or an enemy far away.

MANE
The mane falls down on one side of the neck, and connects at the top of the head to the *forelock*, a bunch of long hair that hangs down toward the horse's eyes.

WITHERS
The high, rounded part of the back above the front legs, called the *withers*, is where a lot of big muscles attach to the backbone.

HEAD
The long head holds a lot of teeth and a large nose with a keen sense of smell.

MAIN LEG JOINT
The main joint on a horse's back leg is the same as the bones of your ankle.

CHEST
A horse's chest is higher than it is wide to hold its large lungs and heart without getting in the way of the motion of running legs.

TAIL
Horses use their long tails to swish away insect pests.

EYES
Horses' eyes are much farther out on the sides of their heads than yours, so they can see danger behind, as well as in front, in time to run away.

HOOVES
Horses stand and move on feet with hooves. A hoof is like one very strong finger and fingernail.

 Tip Understanding how an animal lives helps an artist see it better.

① Add the Body and Leg Wires

Take two long wires and thread them through holes 1 and 5 in two of the round cogs. Let the wires stick out past the cogs—about 3¼ inches for the front legs and about 3½ inches for the rear legs.

Using the large side view of the horse as a guide, bend the wires down to make the legs.

Mark lengths with a pen

3¼ "   3"   3½ "

Use an extra cog to help bend a foot

Tweak...

TIP

To make sharp bends at the bottom of each leg for the horse's feet, use an oval cog as a kind of wrench.

Stick the end of the wire into hole 1 and bend the cog and wire in the direction you want. Remove the cog.

Use an extra cog to help bend a foot

Tweak...

② Add the Head and Tail Wire

Insert a third long wire through both cogs and bend it as shown for the head, neck, and tail.

Compare your armature with this photograph and adjust the wires as needed. Notice that the wire doesn't go all the way to the end of the nose.

fold along the dotted line

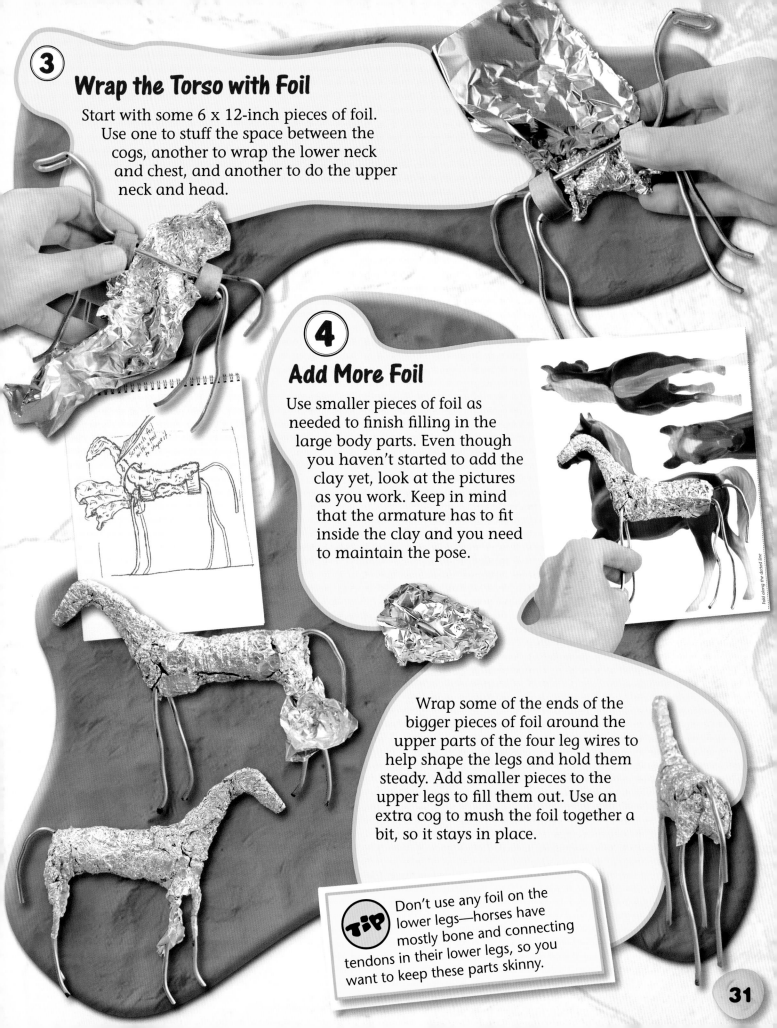

3 Wrap the Torso with Foil

Start with some 6 x 12-inch pieces of foil. Use one to stuff the space between the cogs, another to wrap the lower neck and chest, and another to do the upper neck and head.

4 Add More Foil

Use smaller pieces of foil as needed to finish filling in the large body parts. Even though you haven't started to add the clay yet, look at the pictures as you work. Keep in mind that the armature has to fit inside the clay and you need to maintain the pose.

Wrap some of the ends of the bigger pieces of foil around the upper parts of the four leg wires to help shape the legs and hold them steady. Add smaller pieces to the upper legs to fill them out. Use an extra cog to mush the foil together a bit, so it stays in place.

TIP Don't use any foil on the lower legs—horses have mostly bone and connecting tendons in their lower legs, so you want to keep these parts skinny.

5 Stand the Armature on Its Feet

Tug the armature into the pose you want, then carefully stand it on its feet on the spot you want to finish the sculpture. Put a pea-sized ball of clay around each wire where it touches the base to hold the feet in place.

BORN TO RUN

A horse's body shape is very different from yours, so that the horse can live in the open and always be ready to do what it does best—run. Wild horses run to escape danger, and they travel long distances every day to find food. Although humans have used horses for thousands of years for riding and working, every horse is still a sharp-eyed running machine.

TIP Clay can leave an oily stain on furniture. Always use an "adult-approved" base for your sculptures.

6 Begin Adding Clay

Soften up a whole block of clay by mashing it with your fingers and hands to get it warm, then tear or cut it into walnut-sized pieces.

Mash these pieces to about ¼ inch thick, then start pressing them to the body of the sculpture. Smooth the edges together so the head, neck, and torso are covered, but don't push hard enough to make the clay layer thin.

7

The Neck and Head

Roll a rope of clay. Starting at the shoulders, press the clay all the way around the neck and head armature.

Pinch or cut off extra clay at the end of the nose or on the shoulders where the pieces come together.

8

Upper Legs

Roll a coil of clay and wrap it around the upper legs. Press and smooth the clay until you get the right proportions.

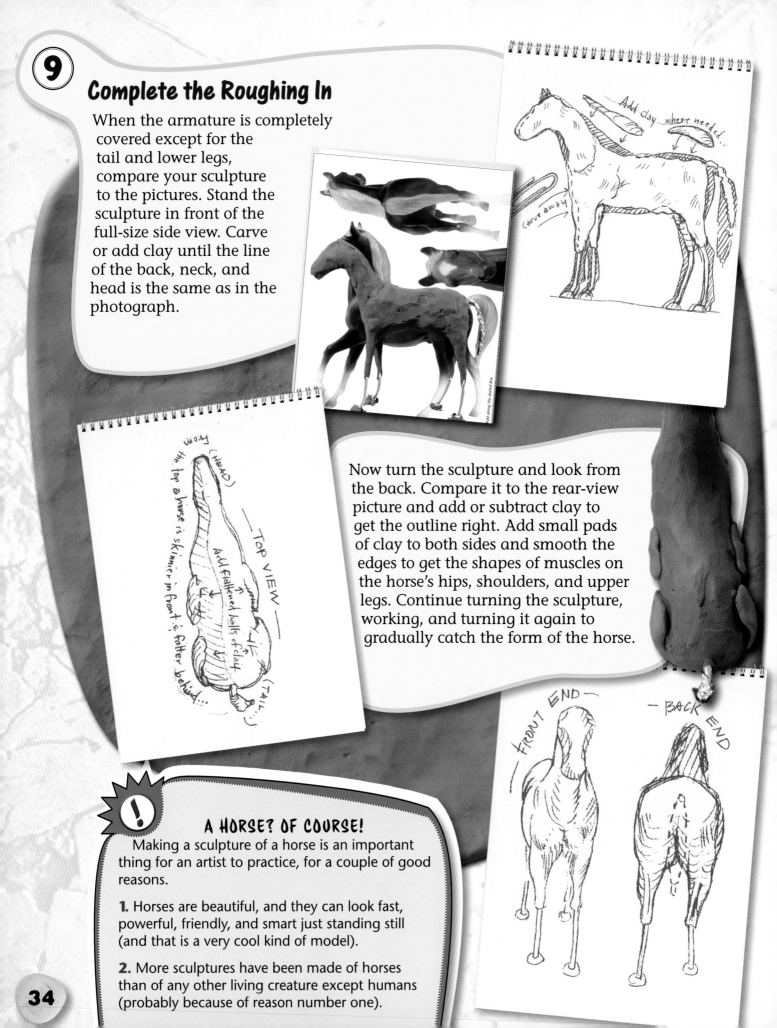

9

Complete the Roughing In

When the armature is completely covered except for the tail and lower legs, compare your sculpture to the pictures. Stand the sculpture in front of the full-size side view. Carve or add clay until the line of the back, neck, and head is the same as in the photograph.

Add clay where needed...

Carve away

TOP VIEW

(HEAD)

(TAIL)

From the top a horse is skinnier in front & fatter behind...

Add flattened balls of clay

Now turn the sculpture and look from the back. Compare it to the rear-view picture and add or subtract clay to get the outline right. Add small pads of clay to both sides and smooth the edges to get the shapes of muscles on the horse's hips, shoulders, and upper legs. Continue turning the sculpture, working, and turning it again to gradually catch the form of the horse.

FRONT END

BACK END

A HORSE? OF COURSE!

Making a sculpture of a horse is an important thing for an artist to practice, for a couple of good reasons.

1. Horses are beautiful, and they can look fast, powerful, friendly, and smart just standing still (and that is a very cool kind of model).

2. More sculptures have been made of horses than of any other living creature except humans (probably because of reason number one).

10 Check Your Work

Check your work by looking at the photographs and your sculpture from different angles.

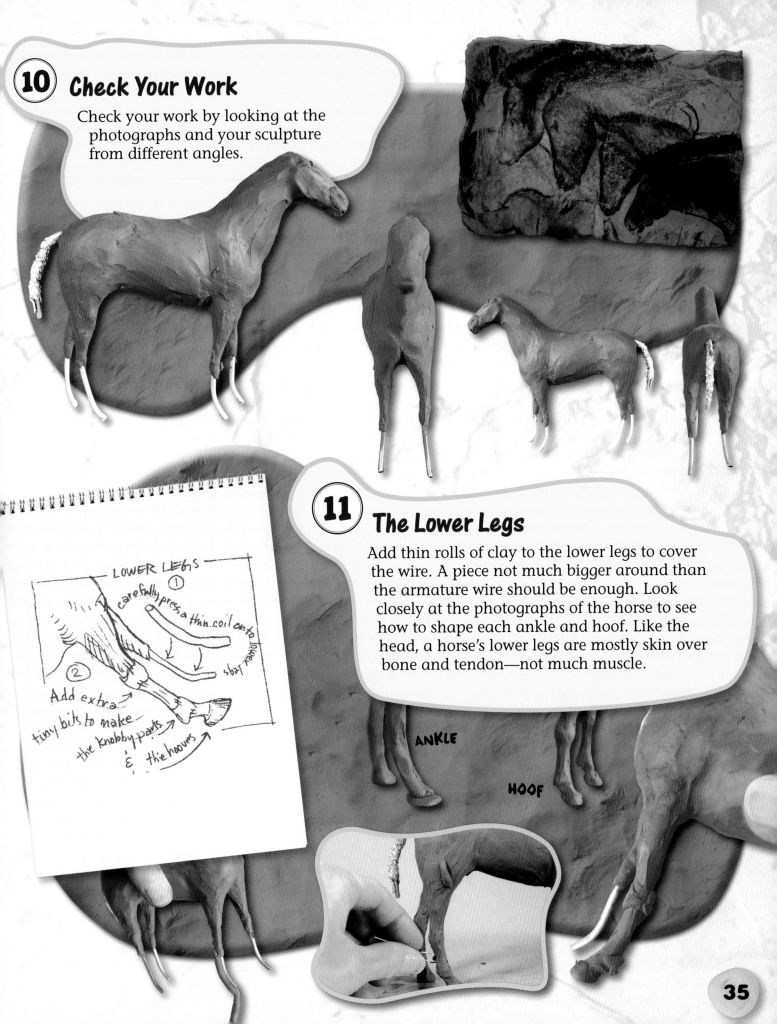

11 The Lower Legs

Add thin rolls of clay to the lower legs to cover the wire. A piece not much bigger around than the armature wire should be enough. Look closely at the photographs of the horse to see how to shape each ankle and hoof. Like the head, a horse's lower legs are mostly skin over bone and tendon—not much muscle.

LOWER LEGS

① carefully press a thin coil onto lower legs

② Add extra tiny bits to make the knobby parts & the hooves

ANKLE

HOOF

(12) The Face

Except around the mouth, a horse's face is quite bony, so you will want to do most of the shaping of the head by carving with a paper clip or other wire. Use the paper clip to carve the muzzle.

Add pads of clay where needed to correct the head shape.

HEAD
Add clay if needed to build up over eyes
Cut away to shape snout & muzzle

TiP Ignore tiny details. This isn't a large sculpture, and the idea is to show the animal's pose and the way its body is put together, so don't worry about tiny details. Often, art that looks "alive" isn't an exact copy of every hair and wrinkle of the model.

The end of the horse's face (the muzzle) is soft, so you don't want to make the lines of the mouth and nostrils look sharp and bony. Put a piece of plastic wrap over the nose and press in with a paper clip or other thin tool to make the mouth line and the two small, curved lines of the nostrils. Then pull the plastic off.

EARS
Finished pair of ears
pinch bottom
cut off

NOSTRILS
Press tool through plastic wrap to make softer marks in clay

(13) The Ears

Cut a pea-sized ball of clay in half to make the ears. Take each half and roll it into a teardrop shape. Use the club-shaped tool to press one side hollow, and then gently smooth the base of the ear onto the horse's head on either side of the highest point, called the *poll*.

(14) The Mane

Press a sheet of clay about the thickness of a coin onto the neck in the mane area. Press a smaller piece between the ears for the forelock.

Using the tip of your spatula tool, press down in slightly wavy lines to give the texture of hair. Follow up with a wire or toothpick for some finer lines (don't press too deep), but don't worry about showing every hair.

(15) The Tail

Cover the wire armature of the tail with clay and texture it like you did the mane.

Ta-DAH!

If you want to keep sculpting, you can make a saddle for your horse, or you can make your horse an Appaloosa by adding small spots of colored clay to its back.

Abstract Sculpture

A Time for Women

As the twentieth century came along, each artist was expected to be different from everyone else, and to have a style of work that was his own and no one else's. One good thing about this new way of thinking was that people who would not have had the chance to be artists in Europe and America could now develop their talent—women, for example.

For centuries, artists tried to create art that looked as much like the real things as possible. However, since reproducing every detail of a real object is impossible, all art has some abstraction, or simplification, to it. In the twentieth century, artists became less interested in portraying fine details and more interested in experimenting with this idea of abstraction.

In abstract art, the artist changes the look of something real, or uses shapes and textures that are straight from the imagination.

Niki de Saint Phalle, *Sun God*, 1983. Stuart Collection, University of California, San Diego.

Niki de Saint Phalle

As a child, Niki de Saint Phalle (1930–2002) was expelled from school for painting all the fig leaves on the school's statues red. By age 18, she was working as a fashion model for American and French magazines. Later, Niki de Saint Phalle became a painter, writer, filmmaker, mother, actor, AIDS activist, and most notably a sculptor. She even created her own perfume. Niki de Saint Phalle's trademark sculptures are colorful, huge, and wildly creative.

"Life... is never the way one imagines it. It surprises you, it amazes you, and it makes you laugh or cry when you don't expect it."

—*Niki de Saint Phalle*

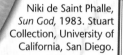

Henry Moore

No artist has more sculptures displayed in public places around the world than the distinguished British sculptor Henry Moore (1898–1986). Although Moore studied classical art and sculpture, he later embraced the forms of abstract art.

"The secret of life is to have a task, something you devote your entire life to, something you bring everything to, every minute of the day for the rest of your life. And the most important thing is, it must be something you cannot possibly do."

—Henry Moore

DOES HENRY MOORE'S ABSTRACT SCULPTURE VERTEBRAE LOOK LIKE BONES TO YOU?

Henry Moore, *Three Piece Sculpture: Vertebrae*, 1968–69 (LH580). Bronze. Reproduced by permission of the Henry Moore Foundation.

Projects

Since the idea of abstract sculpture is so vast, we are going to give you a few suggestions for making abstractions of your own. If you have a different idea for an abstract sculpture project, try it! (Just don't do anything that isn't safe, and don't use things that belong to other people unless you ask them.)

The Maquette

When artists make a small sculpture to try out ideas for a big sculpture, the small one is called a maquette.

Here are some maquettes of the Statue of Liberty by the French sculptor Frédéric-Auguste Bartholdi. Notice how the statue kept changing until the artist found just the right look.

Frédéric-Auguste Bartholdi, six clay models for the Statue of Liberty.

(1) Cubic Abstraction

Make twenty small cubes of clay, each about ½ inch. Imagine that you have been asked to design a sculpture for a park, and you have decided that the sculpture will be a large abstract made of steel cubes. Arrange the clay cubes you have made as a sort of quick sketch or plan for the big sculpture.

Don't change the shape of the cubes; just decide how to put them on or next to each other.

Here are some things to think about:

• People will be looking at your sculpture from the sides. As you put together your clay maquette, don't just look down at it, also look at it from each side.

• The full-size steel sculpture will be welded or bolted together and very sturdy, so you can have the cubes of your maquette stacked up and hanging off each other, if that is part of your design.

Alexander Liberman, *Iliad*, 1954. Storm King Art Center, Mountainville, New York.

② Mystery Abstraction

Find something small that you don't mind getting a little clay stuck to. Make a clay sculpture, using your object as an armature. Don't completely lose the shape of the object, but when you are done, nothing of the object you are using for the armature should show.

Let your imagination build the final form bit by bit. You could use either kind of abstract design: shapes of real things changed or completely new shapes from your imagination—or both.

Use tools, including your fingers, to smooth, texture, and shape the clay you add to the armature. When you are pleased with what you have made, decide on a name for the sculpture. (See if your friends can guess what you started with.)

It didn't look like a dog bone any more, but swirled like water! —VORTEX—

I covered a short chunk of dog bone with clay, inside & out

Then added coils & chunks of clay to some parts, & carved away other areas

③ Conceptual Abstraction

Gently bend a piece of wire into a curve. Use this wire as an armature to build a clay sculpture that you could call *Flying*, but that isn't in the shape of a bird or an airplane. Think about shapes that make you think of leaping, rising, or flying and use your one-wire armature to build those shapes. You could also use a one-wire armature to make a sculpture called *Falling*.

Art: Creating What You Love

You have taken on some challenging projects in this book. You may have liked one project better than the others. If this is true, then perhaps that form of sculpture is the one that inspires you the most, and you will want to take on other projects using that method. Being an artist is all about creating art that you love.

Have fun!

Don Anderson, *Daphnis*, 2004. Welded stainless steel.